ONLY Emma

ONLY
Emma

saLLy WARNER

Illustrated by

jamie HARPeR

SCHOLASTIC INC.

New York   Toronto   London   Auckland   Sydney
Mexico City   New Delhi   Hong Kong   Buenos Aires

ISBN 0-439-82638-1

Text copyright © 2005 by Sally Warner.
Illustrations copyright © 2005 by Jamie Harper. All rights reserved.
Published by Scholastic Inc., 557 Broadway, New York, NY 10012,
by arrangement with Viking Children's Books,
a member of Penguin Group (USA) Inc.
SCHOLASTIC and associated logos are trademarks
and/or registered trademarks of Scholastic Inc.

12 11 10 9 8 7 6 5 4 3 2   6 7 8 9 10/0

Printed in the U.S.A.   40

First Scholastic printing, September 2005

Set in Bitstream Carmina

Book design by Nancy Brennan

For the one and only
Julia Bosley!—S.W.

X   X   X

For Kate—J.H.

Contents

ts

ONLY Emma

❧ 1 ❧

CRAZY ANTHONY

Anthony Scarpetto saw me reaching for that
puzzle piece, but he grabbed it first. And he doesn't
even know where it goes. "Give it," I say to him,
but he does not let me have it.

"You're not the boss of me, Emma McGraw,"
he says, but that's not true. He is only four, and
I am eight, which is twice as much. Of course I
am the boss.

Besides, we're at my house. You are always
the boss—of other kids, anyway—when you are
at your own house. That's the rule, even though
no one ever wrote it down.

Until now.

Why am I even *trying* to do a puzzle with a four-year-old baby on a Sunday night? Because my mom told me I had to be nice to Anthony, that's why. She's friends with his mom and dad. They used to be our neighbors at our old house, before we moved to this condo.

In my opinion, a condo is way worse than a house. You always have to worry about whether or not you are bothering your neighbors, for one thing, even though they never worry about bothering you—with their noise, with the stupid decorations on their porches, with their weird cooking smells.

Other people's cooking is just plain *strange*.

And there are lots of other bad things about living in a condo, but I'm too busy keeping an eye on Anthony to mention them.

My mom and Anthony's mom are sitting in our kitchen right now. They are drinking Constant Comment tea and yak-yak-yakking.

Anthony Scarpetto has black curly hair,

brown eyes, and fat pink cheeks. He is not as cute as he sounds, though—and not nearly as cute as he thinks, even though he is wearing his striped pajamas already. I guess that's so his mom can just stuff him into bed right away to get rid of him when they finally go home.

I am so glad that I do not have a little brother! Or a little sister either, for that matter. I am an only child, and I like it that way.

Only Emma.

"Give it," I say to him again, but I know Anthony is not going to give me the puzzle piece. I'll be lucky if he doesn't eat it just to make me mad.

"Make me," Anthony says. He holds the sticky puzzle piece in the air as if it is a dog biscuit and I am a big old poodle.

I do have curly hair like a poodle, which happens to be a very intelligent dog, in case you

didn't know. My hair is brown, and it comes halfway down my back. Mom says that my hair is so thick that it is hard for her to get a comb through it after a shampoo.

I brush my own hair the rest of the time, but

sometimes—I admit it—I just skim the brush over the outermost hairs on my head so that they look okay.

That's my basic approach to a lot of things, actually.

I wish my hair was smooth and shiny all the time, like Cynthia Harbison's. Cynthia is my best friend at my new school, even though I know she wouldn't say the same thing about me.

But Cynthia's mom can get a comb through her hair easy as pie, probably.

I shrug my shoulders. "Keep the puzzle piece, then," I say to Anthony. "I don't care. I don't even like that puzzle. I was just trying to be nice to you."

I *do* like the puzzle, though. It shows an orange cat—a boy—curled up next to a pumpkin, fast asleep. The *cat* is fast asleep, I mean, not the pumpkin.

Did you know that almost all orange cats are boys? It's true. And cats that are three colors—

white, black, and brown—are usually always girls.

It's *science.*

"Show me where it goes," Anthony says, scowling. He tries to push the piece into the wrong place. He is putting kitty fur in the sky! The bumpy part of the cardboard puzzle piece bends, of course. And I hate it when puzzle pieces bend. It reminds me of sprained ankles.

"Stop, you're wrecking it," I say. "That's a very valuable puzzle."

It isn't, but he doesn't know that.

"You just said you didn't like it," Anthony reminds me.

"I don't," I lie. "But that doesn't mean that I want to see you ruining it."

"Then show me where it goes," Anthony says again.

I could do what he wants, but then Anthony will just grab the next puzzle piece I reach for, so why bother? And anyway, I am tired of playing with him. He is giving me a little headache.

Besides, it's not as though we're really playing together. When kids play, they're supposed to have fun. This is not fun.

This is something else.

"Nuh-uh," I tell Anthony. "Figure it out yourself if you're so smart. I'm busy." I get up, walk over to my bookcase, and look at the nature

books there as if they are the most interesting things in the world. Which they are, by the way.

"But you *have* to play with me. Mommy said," Anthony yells, jumping up so fast that the white wicker chair he was sitting in clunks sideways to the ground. Now, his face is pink all over.

"No one can make me do anything I don't want to do," I tell him. "Anyway," I say, "it's my room. Don't go knocking over the chair in my room. *Please*." I add the *please* to be polite. And just in case my mom is listening.

Now, Anthony's face is almost red, he is so angry. "I can knock over anything I want," he says. To prove it, he swings his arm back, and he sweeps the whole puzzle—that *could* have been valuable, he doesn't know!—off the table and onto the floor.

The box says that there are seventy-five pieces in that puzzle, and all seventy-five pieces go flying everywhere. Two or three of them stick to the arm of Anthony's pajamas like magnets.

"Oh, great," I tell him. "Well, you'll just have to pick the pieces up, that's all. And I'm counting every single one, so you'd better get started."

"No *way*," Anthony squawks, and he starts hopping up and down, stomping on the puzzle pieces. He turns into a red-and-white-striped blur.

So here I am, holding a book about birds in one hand while a strange four-year-old kid is going bonkers in my bedroom. He's wrecking my stuff!

I don't know what to do.

I am a girl who likes peace and quiet, at least when I'm at home. But there will be no peace and quiet as long as Anthony Scarpetto is around, I am thinking.

My mom pops her head through the doorway, *finally*. "What's going on in here?" she says.

She's asking *me*? I'm just standing here in my own room, minding my own business! "You'd

better ask Mr. Big Baby Snit-Fit over there," I say, pointing to Anthony.

Anthony is still stomping puzzle pieces, but not as hard as before. It's as if he is some weird Christmas toy, and a few of his double-A batteries are running down.

"Anthony, honey?" my mom says, using her soft voice. She kneels down and holds out her arms.

"*Wah-h-h-h-h,*" Anthony cries, and he runs into my mother's hug so hard that he knocks her over. I don't like to see her hug Anthony. Where's *his* mom, anyway? It is her job to hug this terrible kid.

I mean, I feel sorry for her and everything, but tough.

"Oof," Mom says, and she laughs and gives little striped Anthony another big squeeze.

Tears are squirting out of Anthony's eyes as though he has a sprinkler turned on inside, the big faker. "Emma wouldn't play with me," Anthony says. He is such a tattletale.

"You call that *playing?*" I ask, and I point to the puzzle disaster all over my floor.

"Simmer down, you two," my mother says. "Emma, let's get this picked up."

"Okay," I say, "but Anthony has to help, at least." Anthony snuffles and wipes his nose on his pajama sleeve.

Yuck. That is so typical of him.

"I don't wanna help," Anthony says, sliding me a look.

"He doesn't have to help," Mom says. "I want Anthony to go into the kitchen, Em. His mother needs to talk to him."

Anthony gives me a secret *hah-hah-on-you* kind of grin.

"But *Mom*," I say. This is very bad for him!

"Go on, Anthony—she's waiting for you," my mother tells him. And Anthony goes pattering off down the hall.

"That's so not fair," I say. "He made this mess."

My mom is already picking up the pieces. "You two are going to have to learn how to get along, Emma," she tells me. "Just because you don't have any brothers or sisters, that doesn't mean you can't—"

"But I *was* getting along," I say. I am interrupting her, but this is important. "Anthony is the one who wouldn't play right," I tell her. "He was pounding puzzle pieces into the wrong places—with his bare fist!"

"He's only four," Mom reminds me, scooping up some more puzzle pieces.

I am starting to feel even angrier than before. "Well, anyway," I say, "I don't *have* to learn how to get along with crazy Anthony, because he will be going home in about one minute. Thank goodness."

"I wanted to talk with you about that," Mom says, and she settles back as though we are about to have a cozy little chat.

I do not want to have a chat with her tonight. I just want to be left alone—in my nice, quiet, picked-up room. That's all.

I have library books about insects that I need to read.

So I don't say anything.

I can hear Anthony crying again, though—in the kitchen, this time.

"Anthony will be staying with us for a little while, Emma," Mom says, her voice soft. "For at least a week, actually."

"What?" I yell. I can't help it.

My mom pats her hands in the air like that is going to calm things down. "Shhh," she says. "Anthony's grandmother in Tucson is very sick, sweetie, and his mom and dad are going to go help take care of her."

"So why can't Anthony go, too?" I ask, trying to make my voice sound normal. "His grandmother probably thinks he's *darling*. It would do her good to see him."

"He would just be in the way," Mom says.

I can believe that much, at least.

"Emma?" Mom says.

I don't answer.

My mother waves her hands in front of my eyes, then lifts up some of my curly hair and pretends to peer inside my ear. "Anyone home in there?" she asks, trying to make a joke.

"When?" I ask her. The word comes out croaky. "When do we have to start taking care of him?"

"Right away, darling," Mom replies. "Anthony's mother brought his little duffel bag with her. She's explaining the situation to him now."

Which must be the reason

he's crying. "You mean he's staying here *tonight?*" I ask, horrified. "But where will he sleep?"

My mom looks over at my guest bed, the one where my new friend Cynthia sleeps when she stays over. Which has only been once so far, because school just started.

"In my room?" I yell.

Down the hall, Anthony is still sobbing.

Hey, I know just how he feels! I'd sob, too, only I'm too old.

"It's just for a little while," Mom says. She snaps the lid closed on the puzzle box as though she is saying, *That's final.*

"Well, it's going to seem like a whole lot longer," I tell her.

Because she might be the mom, but already, I know a thing or two about Anthony.

x 2 x

Poor Little Guy

It is morning!

Finally.

I thought the sun would never come up.

Anthony huffled and snuffled like a baby wart hog for about an hour before he fell asleep last night. I tried to make him feel better. I said, "Look, Anthony, your mom and dad will come back as soon as they can. I'm sure they won't decide to take a vacation all by themselves while they have the chance. And they won't forget where they left you."

"*Wah-h-h-h,*" Anthony yelled.

I guess I should have kept my big mouth shut and not tried to comfort him.

But if I was a mom and I had a noisy little kid like Anthony, I might *want* to forget where I left him.

Now, though, Anthony is still asleep. He was yelping with bad dreams all night, which is why I have dark circles under my eyes.

Anthony is lying on my guest bed as though someone threw him there. His red-and-white-striped pajama legs are all tangled up in the pink sheets.

He clashes with my room.

And—he's drooling on my guest-bed pillow!

Well, that's just gross. I hope Cynthia doesn't find out.

I tiptoe over to my closet and get out the clothes I want to wear to school today. I will have to change in the bathroom.

This stinks. I can't even get dressed in my own room anymore!

But my friend Cynthia and I talked on the phone yesterday afternoon, as usual, and we both decided to wear green today, so that's good. Especially since I have a brand-new green top.

Perfect!

Today is going to be so much fun, with us wearing practically the same clothes. I am lucky I found a friend so fast after changing schools. Finding your first friend at a new school is like discovering a life preserver floating past your nose when you're right in the middle of drowning. You're safe, at least for a while.

I open the bureau drawer to get my underwear. *Oh no.* The drawer squeaks. I am scared to turn around, in case the noise has made you-know-who wake up.

But when I look, Anthony is lying there, watching me with sleepy brown eyes. "What are you doing?" he asks.

"Getting my clothes, obviously," I say. "I'll tell Mom you're ready to get up. Just stay right where you are. Don't move a muscle."

And hearing those words, of course, Anthony springs out of bed like a jackrabbit. I saw a nature program about them once—or was it about Siberian hares?—on PBS.

Jackrabbits can leap 15 to 20 feet in a single bound.

I love nature programs; they are my favorite. Except when they go too slow, like when someone says, *"And now the icy fingers of winter touch Yosemite Valley,"* or when something little and furry gets killed—in slow motion. Slow motion is always bad news in the animal kingdom.

"I'm up," Anthony says, as if this is the greatest news he could tell me.

He smells like peanut butter, even from across the room, I notice—and even this early in the morning.

I guess it's a boy thing.

"Well, follow me," I say, and we march down the hall to the kitchen. My mom is on the phone, but she says good-bye in a great big hurry when she sees the look on my face. "Here he is," I say when she has hung up.

Why can't Anthony Scarpetto sleep in *her* room, if she likes him so much?

"Come here, you," my mother says tenderly to Anthony, opening her arms wide.

I don't stay to see the rest of this revolting scene. I lock myself in the bathroom and start to get ready for school.

I used to go to Magdalena School, which is private, girls only. Now, I go to Oak Glen Primary School, which is public. Girls and boys. I am in the third grade, which lasts all day long, naturally. My teacher's name is Ms. Sanchez. She is so pretty that she could be on a TV show.

Anthony goes to afternoon preschool.

Oak Glen is the name of our town, too. It is in California, an hour north of San Diego. Our town is not on the ocean, though—it's in the hills.

"Breakfast is ready," Mom tells me through the bathroom door. "It's safe, Emma, you can come out now." She sounds as though she is making a joke.

Ha ha, very funny.

"It's safe? Why? Did Anthony run away or something?" I ask her through the door.

"No, but he's busy watching *Sesame Street*," Mom says.

"Promise?" I say, peeking out.

My mom looks me up and down. "That green top is even cuter on," she says, and I feel better all of a sudden, thinking about how much fun Cynthia and I will have today. Because wearing something you really like—and that looks good on you—can make an ordinary day fabulous.

Mom and I sneak into the kitchen, and she puts some scrambled eggs and toast on a plate for me. I can hear Big Bird in the other room, and Anthony is singing along, not very well.

"How did it go with Anthony last night?" Mom asks, pouring some coffee into her mug.

"Mmm, okay, I guess," I say slowly. I want her to at least *think* that I am trying to be a good sport. "But he breathes too loud," I add. "He sort of snuffles and snorts." Usually it's just my mom and me, and things are pretty quiet around our house. See, my dad moved away when I was two years old—which is why I am an only child.

You do the math.

(Whatever *that* means.)

Mom looks worried. "He snuffles? Gee, I hope he's not catching a cold," she says, fretting.

"He isn't," I reassure her. "I think his nose was just stuffy from all that crying." Anthony's nose is not huge, but it seems to be very runny.

Which can be quite disgusting, actually.

"Poor little guy," Mom says, then she sighs.

And I am thinking, *What about poor little me?*

"I'm thirsty," Anthony calls from the door-way.

"I'll get you some juice, honey-bunny," Mom says.

Honey-bunny. Terrific.

Anthony looks at me in my brand-new green top. "You look like a great big grasshopper," he says, tilting his head as if *he* were the nature scientist.

Which is what I want to be when I grow up, in case you couldn't figure that out!

I look down at my top, which suddenly does not seem so wonderful any-more.

"Emma does not look like a grasshopper at all, Anthony," Mom says. I can tell that she is trying not to smile, though, which makes everything worse.

"I meant that her *shirt* looks like—"

"I know, I know, it looks like a great big grasshopper," I say, finishing the awful sentence for him. "Although for your information, it's a *top*, not a shirt." I turn to Mom. "Do I have time to change?"

"No," Mom says, and she grabs her car keys and hands me my lunch. "We have to scoot," she says. She takes Anthony by the hand.

"Does he have to come, too?" I ask, but I say it under my breath. Because I already know the answer.

"Of course he does, Emma. Did you think I'd leave a four-year-old child all alone in the house?"

"It's a *condo*," I mumble.

"Yay, I get to ride in the car in my PJs," he says, jumping up and down.

The weirdest things make him happy!

"Promise me you won't let him out of the car?" I ask my mom. I try not to sound as though I am begging, but it is hard.

She crosses her heart and nods, without saying any words.

But that's good enough for me. At least Anthony won't get a chance to embarrass me in front of the whole school by prancing around in his PJs and possibly bursting into tears for no reason.

Boy, I think, *this must be just like having a real little brother.*

What a terrible thought!

I guess I should count my blessings, the way Mom always says.

tHere are No KoaLas iN Oak GLeN, CaLiforNia

"Who was that in the car with you and your mom?" Cynthia asks me. She is wearing bright green skinny-leg pants, a pure white T-shirt with lace trim, and a green plastic headband with sparkles trapped inside.

"Nobody," I tell her, smoothing down my new green top. I don't know why, but I want to keep Anthony private. At least for now.

Cynthia and I walk across the patio to our classroom door, crunching eucalyptus leaves. They are curved like little brown moons. Koalas eat eucalyptus leaves, and *only* eucalyptus

leaves, but there are no koalas in Oak Glen, California. That doesn't seem right. Couldn't nature have planned things better than that?

There are some koalas in the San Diego Zoo, though, and that's not too far away.

Koalas are not bears, by the way, even

Koalas
ONLY eat
eucalyptus
leaves.

though people say "koala bear" all the time. They're marsupials, which means they have pouches. Like kangaroos.

"Oh," Cynthia says, accepting my strange answer to her question.

We get to the classroom door, and I let her walk in first. Some kids are already sitting down.

Cynthia leans over to whisper something to me. "My mom says it's fine about Friday," she tells me, as if it is a great big secret. She opens her mouth a little and smiles, as though she is waiting for me to say *Yippee*.

"Friday?" I say, staring at her. What is she talking about? I can't remember. I feel stupid, but I try to make my face look smart.

"You know," she says, frowning suddenly, "when you come sleep over at *my* house."

"Oh, yeah," I say. "That'll be fun." I try to match her smile. I can't believe I forgot about the

best thing that has happened to me in a long, long time.

"Wait a minute. Did you even ask your mom?" Cynthia asks, suspicious now.

"I—I meant to," I tell her. "Only things got kind of goofed up at our house last night." *Thanks a lot, Anthony*, I think.

"You don't even care about coming over,"

Cynthia says, flinging herself into her seat so hard that her green plastic headband flies off.

I pick it up and hand it to her. She grabs it from me. "I do too care," I say.

"Hmmph," she says, jamming the headband back onto her head.

"Quiet down, everyone, while I read our Monday morning announcements," Ms. Sanchez is saying.

Her reading the announcements gives me time to think. *Do* I care about going over to Cynthia's? Yes! I want to sleep over there on Friday night. She's my best—and only!—friend at Oak Glen, my new school, even though she can be a little grouchy. And going to her house would give me some time away from you-know-who.

If I went to Cynthia's right after school on Friday, and if I stayed until late Saturday afternoon, that would be almost two whole Anthony-free days.

Perfect!

Except then I would miss whatever crazy thing Anthony did next, or some funny thing that he might say.

I surprise myself by thinking this.

"Emma?" Ms. Sanchez is saying. Uh-oh, she is tapping her pencil on her desk.

Cynthia nudges me, and I stand up. "Yes?" I say.

"I was asking if you'd like to pass out these flyers about the PTA candy sale," Ms. Sanchez says, frowning.

"Oh. Sure," I tell her, and I stumble to her desk as if my feet are asleep.

Usually I love doing things for Ms. Sanchez, but not when she's in a bad mood. So now Ms. Sanchez is mad at me, and Cynthia is, too.

And it's all because of Anthony Scarpetto.

When I sit down again, it is word-list time. We are supposed to work with partners: first one kid, and then another kid.

For me, the first kid is Corey Robinson. He

has freckles all over his face, and greeny-yellow hair from spending so much time in the swimming pool. Chlorine can do that to a person. "Okay," he says, looking down at a sheet of paper, "spell *'with,'* and use it in a sentence."

"'With,'" I say. "W-I-T-H. *I am bored with this."*

Corey looks at me and grins. "You'd better not let Ms. Sanchez hear you," he says, peering over his shoulder.

"Why not?" I say, sounding brave. "I used the word right, didn't I?"

"I guess," Corey says, looking doubtful. "Okay, the next word is *'these,'"* he says.

I'm not so sure about the word *"these,"* but I like showing off for Corey. *"'These,'"* I say slowly. "T-H-E-S. *These are very stupid words."*

Corey peeks up as if he is afraid to tell me some bad news. "You spelled it wrong," he says. Corey looks a little like Anthony when he is scared, I notice.

His comment makes me frown. "No I didn't," I tell him. "Are you sure?"

"Yeah, it has two *Es*," he says, looking as though he is sorry to have to be the one to tell me.

I frown some more. "T-H-E-E-S? That doesn't sound right," I say.

"Change partners," Ms. Sanchez calls out, as though we are folk dancing in the gym. I wish we *were* folk dancing! At least we would be having some fun that way—although the one time our class tried it, we got mixed up and crashed into each other in the middle of the room. This girl named Heather got a bloody nose and had to go to the nurse.

Folk dancing can be dangerous.

I turn my back on Corey, who is just trying to trick me about how to spell "*these*," probably.

Now my partner is Cynthia. I'm supposed to ask *her* the words. "Okay, '*which*,'" I say to her.

Cynthia sniffs and sticks her nose in the air

like a cartoon lady who has smelled a skunk. "'*Which*,'" she announces. "W-I-C-H," she says. She tries to sound as if she knows she's right.

I do not want to inform her that she is wrong, so I don't. "Use it in a sentence," I remind her.

"I know, I know," she says, cranky. She thinks for a few seconds. "*A witch is a person who forgets about going over to her friend's house*," she says at last.

Oh no—she means me! And not only that, but Cynthia has her *whiches* mixed up. I don't want to be the one to tell her, though. "Correct," I say like a teacher. I swoop my tangly hair back behind my ears the way Ms. Sanchez does and then pretend that I am admiring my engagement ring. Ms. Sanchez does that, too.

Phew! Cynthia can't help it—she starts to giggle.

"Emma?" a quiet voice behind me says.

Oh, no! It's the real Ms. Sanchez. How long has she been standing there? Did she see me

gazing at my pretend engagement ring? "Yes?" I almost whisper the word.

"It's not the Halloween kind of witch, it's the other kind," my teacher says to me, as if I didn't know. "And Cynthia didn't spell either word right," she continues. "You're supposed to be checking that list, or else this exercise is just a waste of time."

"I—I lost my place," I fib. "I'll be more careful from now on."

Ms. Sanchez glides off to help somebody else, and all that is left behind is the smell of flowers.

She shouldn't sneak around like that. I think she should wear bells around her ankle or something.

"How do you really spell it?" Cynthia whispers to me.

"W–H–I–C–H," I say, whispering back. "Like in _Which way are you going?_"

I'm good at words.

"I'm sorry I called you the other word," Cynthia says, rolling her pencil under the palm of her hand. _Rrrrr, rrrr, rrrr._

"That's okay," I say. "But I didn't forget about going over to your house," I add.

"So you'll ask your mom tonight?" Cynthia says.

I nod my head. _I sure will_, the nod tells her.

"And _we're_ still friends?" Cynthia asks shyly.

I nod my head again. We sure are!

✗ 4 ✗

a Pain in the Patootie

"Rrrrr, rrrrr, rrrrr," Anthony growls under his breath as he scoots his metal truck across the kitchen floor. The truck reaches one of my feet, stops for a second, then rolls right over it. *"Rrrrr."*

"Ow, quit it," I yell.

"That didn't even hurt," Anthony informs me. He rolls the truck into the hall.

"How do you know whether it hurt or not?" I call after him. "It's my foot!"

It *didn't* hurt, as a matter of fact, but only because I am wearing my sneakers. Anthony doesn't know that, though. He should learn to be more careful.

Mom pokes her head around the corner. "Are you guys all right in here?"

"Well, I'm trying to do my homework," I tell her. "But wherever I go, Anthony follows me."

Secretly, I am proud of this. I am an Anthony-magnet.

"The little guy likes you," my mom says, beaming.

"Huh," I say. I am trying to be modest, but it does make me feel kind of good. In a weird way.

"Did the timer go off yet?" Mom asks.

"Nuh-uh," I say. Its *ticka-ticka-ticka* noise bounces around the kitchen, and the yummy smells of dinner fill the air.

"Well, tell me when it rings," Mom says.

"When what rings?" Anthony asks, chugging back into the room with his truck. "The telephone? Is it my mommy and daddy?" He looks around the kitchen as if they might be standing there.

"Oh, no, honey—not yet," Mom says. "I'm sorry." She holds out her arms to him, and sure enough, he bursts into tears.

It's as though there's a boo-hoo switch inside him or something.

"I want to ask you a question," I say to my mom over the terrible racket Anthony is making.

"Excuse me?" she asks. She cups her hand to her ear to show me that she can't hear what I just said.

"I want to *ask* you something," I shout.

The kitchen timer goes off with its scary little buzz. That timer always surprises Mom and me, no

matter how much we think we are expecting it to ring.

We all jump. "*Wah-h-h-h,*" Anthony cries even louder.

"Can what you want to say wait until later?" Mom yells at me.

"I guess it'll have to," I yell back, mad.

✕ ✕ ✕

After dinner, it is time for Anthony's bath. I try to get as far away from the bathroom as possible, because I do not care to see a bare little boy staggering around like a robot. I already saw that five minutes ago.

Yuck.

When Anthony is in the bathtub, it sounds as though there are lots of creatures in there with him—growly bears, squeaky bats, and two or three other kids. He makes a lot of noise for someone who is only four.

The bathroom door is open, and Mom is rearranging sheets and stuff in the hall closet. She wants to give him some privacy, but I guess she is afraid he might fall and bump his head.

I think he probably won't. Maybe we should close the door, give him a *lot* of privacy, and take our chances.

(I'm only kidding.)

Finally, Mom stuffs him into my guest bed for another night of sniffling and snuffling. I don't have to go to bed yet, though, because I'm older. My mom leaves the light on in my closet so he won't be scared.

He is singing Christmas carols as loud as he can, even though it is still September. I guess he is trying to cheer himself up.

Poor little guy, like my mom says.

"I want to ask you something," I tell Mom again. "It's important."

"Okay," she says, sighing. She looks very tired, and her shirt is wet from Anthony's bath. We sit down in the living room, as if we are our own guests.

Maybe we should have a tea party, while we're at it!

I say *ahem* first, like they do in the funnies. "Cynthia Harbison invited me over to her house on Friday," I say to my mom. "I forgot to ask permission before."

Mom smiles. "Do you mean she wants you to come play after school?" she asks.

"Nuh-uh," I say, shaking my head. "She wants me to spend the night."

"Oh, Emma," Mom says, "can't that wait for a week? Because what about poor little Anthony?"

"I never slept over at Cynthia's house before in my whole life," I say, trying not to whine.

"And she's my first friend since you made me change schools. And I don't *care* about poor little Anthony."

I mean those last few words when I say them, but only for a second.

"I'm sure you care about him, sweetheart," my mom tells me, as if she can read my mind. She ignores what I said about changing schools, which was all her fault for losing her job.

Magdalena was a very expensive school.

"But since you've never stayed with Cynthia," Mom says, "a week wouldn't be too much longer to wait, would it?"

"She said it had to be this Friday," I tell her. "And I thought you wanted me to make new friends."

"Well, I do. And I won't say no, Emma, but I really want you to think about it," Mom says. "I think Anthony needs the two of us. Just listen to him."

I am making a scrunchy face by now, but I

listen. Anthony is singing "Jingle Bells" for about the millionth time, but by now he is yelling *"Jim–bull Gells"* instead, and his voice is all scratchy.

I have to say that sometimes Anthony is a pain in the patootie.

Somebody said that about *me* once, but it was a long time ago. I outgrew it.

"So what?" I say to Mom, referring to all that singing. "That's a good reason for me to get out of here, isn't it?"

My mom takes one of my hands in hers. "Come on, Em," she says. Now, *she's* the one who sounds a little whiny. "I need your help, honey. This is a really tough time for the little guy, and he seems to like having you around."

I don't get it. First she wants to take care of Anthony, and now she acts like she's scared to be alone with him. "Well, what about me?" I shout, jumping up and yanking my hand away. "What about what *I* like? It's bad enough that you don't even have a regular job anymore and that we had to move to such a teensy place. Now we have to take care of a baby who's not even ours, too?"

Mom looks the same way she did that time when she couldn't get the tape out of the VCR. "Come on," she says again, finally. "Things aren't that terrible for us here, Emma. And Anthony's not so bad, is he?"

I put my hands on my hips and stomp my foot. "Yes, he is," I say. "He *is* so bad."

Mom puts her finger to her lips, but it is too late—the singing has stopped.

In fact, Anthony is standing in the hall, looking at us. His face looks like a round white marshmallow under all that curly black hair.

And he is crying— without making a sound.

For once.

5

Uh-Oh

"I'm a bad boy," Anthony tells me the next morning at breakfast. He scowls.

My mom is putting some clothes in the washing machine, so she doesn't hear what he is saying.

"Why?" I ask him. "What did you do?" I take a bite of my cornflakes.

He looks lost for a second. "Nothing," he finally says. "I guess I'm just bad, that's all."

"No, you're not," I say to him.

"I am too. You said," he tells me. "Last night. I heard you. Don't lie."

"I'm not lying," I say. I can feel my face get hot,

though. I feel terrible that Anthony overheard what I said, but that wasn't really my fault. "I didn't say you were bad, Anthony. I said you were *that bad*. There's a big difference, you know."

Anthony chomps down hard on his toast and frowns some more, thinking. "What's the big difference?" he finally asks. Crumbs fly everywhere.

"It's too complicated to explain," I tell him, as

if this is a third-grade thing that preschoolers could never, ever understand.

When, really, I can't figure out what the difference is fast enough to tell him.

Anthony bites his toast again and chews hard. He reminds me of this other nature program I saw once, about termites. It was a little bit nauseating, to be perfectly honest.

But I'm working on liking insects better, even the yucky ones. After all, if I want to be a scientist some day, I have to give bugs a chance, at least.

Anthony takes a drink of milk. "Well, if I'm so good, where are my mommy and daddy?"

"Huh?" I ask him. "They're taking care of your grandmother in Tucson, that's where they are."

"And if I'm so good," he continues, ignoring my words, "how come you never want to play with me?"

Termites work 24 hours a day. They never sleep.

I stir a circle in my cornflakes, which are all soggy, by the way—I don't care what any commercial says. "I play with you," I remind him.

"Yeah, when your mom makes you," he says gloomily. His pink cheeks stand out on his white face like clown paint—only he is not laughing the way a clown does.

I decide to explain things to him another way. "Listen, Anthony, don't you have *other* friends you like to play with?" I ask him. "Friends in preschool?"

"Yeah, but I can't invite them over. Not when I'm living here, at your house," he says. He slurps down some more milk.

That actually makes sense, I think, kind of surprised. After all, those kids' parents don't know my mom and me. Why would they let their kids play at some stranger's condo, even if it was with Anthony?

Mom comes into the kitchen with clean clothes neatly folded in a yellow plastic laundry basket. "You'd better get a move on, Emma," she says, looking up at the kitchen clock.

"Okay," I say, but when I carry my cereal bowl to the sink, it feels as though I am a hippopotamus walking through mud, I am so tired.

Like I said, I did not get very much sleep last night.

That's what happens when you hurt somebody's feelings.

✕ ✕ ✕

I get to Oak Glen Primary School before Cynthia does, and that is at least one thing to be glad about. Mom was going to call Cynthia's mother last night, to thank her for the invitation. But I told her *I* wanted to be the one to tell Cynthia what I would do on Friday.

The truth is, though, I don't know what I am going to do, or what I am going to say to Cynthia.

I guess Mom could tell I had mixed feelings about Cynthia's invitation. She said that I could invite Cynthia over to my house instead, on Friday night, and we could have a slumber party—with Anthony.

Oh, yeah, right. That sounds like fun.

I wait in the cloak room like a trapdoor spider about to pounce on its prey—only I'm a whole lot cuter, I hope. Finally, Cynthia dashes in to hang up her sweater. I grab her arm.

Trapdoor spiders live in holes in the ground. They spin traps of silk + soil.

"Yow," Cynthia squeals, and then she laughs. "You scared me," she says.

"I have to talk to you about something," I whisper in her ear.

"Young ladies?" a voice says. It is Ms. Sanchez.

I think she calls us "young ladies" sometimes,

instead of "girls," because then we might use better manners in class. She calls the boys "gentlemen," too, even Jared and Stanley. And that's stretching things a little.

Ms. Sanchez is a person who expects the best from people.

"Yes-s-s-s?" Cynthia and I say together, like talking snakes.

"It's time to sit down," she says, tapping at her watch.

Cynthia and I follow Ms. Sanchez into the classroom. Part of me feels like saying *phew*—because Cynthia gets huffy very fast, and I do not want her to be mad at me because of what I decide about Friday.

If it's not the decision she wants me to make, I mean.

Ms. Sanchez takes a few minutes to read us the school announcements, so I have some extra time to think about what to do. I *could* invite Cynthia over to my house, the way Mom said, except I really, really do not think that Cynthia is the type of person who would like Anthony Scarpetto. Cynthia is an only child, just like me—but if *she* saw Anthony running around with no clothes on, she would probably faint right on the floor.

And then everyone at my new school would hear all about it, and I would be totally embar-rassed.

Or I could go spend the night at Cynthia's house, and forget all about Anthony. He might

be sad, true, but it's not as though he would starve or anything.

Except then I remember the look on Mom's face when she asked me to stay home.

And of course, I remember Anthony.

Oh, why didn't Mom just tell me that I *had* to stay home on Friday night? How come she told me I could make up my own mind about it? No fair!

Which brings me to the third choice I could make, of course, which is staying home: just me, my mom, and Anthony. Even if Anthony *is* a pain in the patootie.

I can't help it—I sigh so hard that the person sitting in front of me turns around and makes a face. "Quit it," he mutters, smoothing down his hair as though a hot Santa Ana wind just messed it up.

"You quit it," I say back, even though I know saying that doesn't make any sense.

" . . . subtraction," Ms. Sanchez says, finishing

a sentence. She is standing in front of the blackboard with a piece of chalk in her hand. "Now, who would like to come to the board to demonstrate?"

Uh-oh, I think. *I'd better start paying attention.*

Some sea anemones live for 100 years.

When Ms. Sanchez asks for a volunteer, all the kids in class shrink back into their chairs like sea anemones—which I also saw once, on the Animal Planet. *Not me, not me*, everyone is thinking.

We are having a little trouble with the subtraction of large numbers in my class.

"Corey," Ms. Sanchez says, smiling as though she's just found the little plastic prize in a box of Cracker Jacks.

Next to me, poor Corey Robinson shudders and moans so softly that only I can hear him. "Go on," I whisper, nudging him with my elbow. "You can do it."

But he can't, not really. Not yet. You should see his worksheets! There are holes in them, from his erasing them so hard.

Corey stumbles to the blackboard like Frankenstein's monster, takes the chalk from Ms. Sanchez, drops it, then picks it up again. His zillions of freckles look as if they are about to jump off his suddenly pale face and make a run for the door.

I wait for Corey to drop the chalk again. Maybe he thinks he can just keep right on doing that, over and over again, until the recess bell rings. That will probably be his strategy.

Hey, that's funny, I think. Corey wants recess to happen *right now*, and I'm scared for it to happen at all.

Because what am I going to tell Cynthia about Friday night?

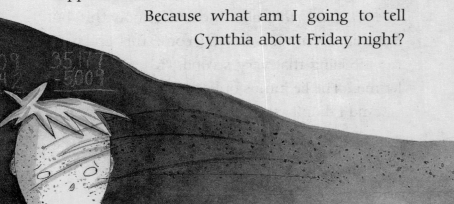

✗ 6 ✗

SCREECH!

"So, what time are you coming over on Friday?" Cynthia asks me. It is recess, and we are lying on our stomachs on the last two swings. My curly hair is hanging down in my eyes. I have been pretending that it is seaweed, and that I am a marine biologist. Back and forth, back and forth, we swing at exactly the same time. And that's not easy.

Back and forth is about to end. I know this, but Cynthia doesn't. "I—I can't come this Friday," I say, deciding that very second. "My mom won't let me." The lie jumps out of my mouth.

And I didn't even know it was in there!

Screech! Sure enough, Cynthia digs the toes of her shoes into the sand. "Well, how come?" she asks, scrambling to her feet. She looks like a highway patrol guy on TV who is about to take someone in for questioning

"Well, there's this little boy staying with us for a while," I say, "and I have to babysit him. So Mom told me I had to stay home." I stand up and brush sand off my knees.

Cynthia puts her hands on her hips, and her eyes get skinny. "You're too young to be a baby-sitter," she says, frowning. "Who is it? That kid who was in your car yesterday?"

I nod, looking very sad.

"I thought you said that was nobody," Cynthia says.

"He *is* nobody," I tell her in a hurry. "He's just Anthony Scarpetto. And I'm not babysitting him all by myself," I add. "But Mom says I have to help her take care of him. Just us, and nobody else. Can't I come over next week, instead?"

I want her to say, *"Yes, of course, because you are my best friend!"*

"I don't know," Cynthia says, kicking at the sand. "Next week is a long time from now. I'm not sure what I'll be doing then."

Or who she'll be friends with, maybe.

I would tell Cynthia that next week is not a *very* long time from now, but it is time to go back to class.

Again.

Work, recess, work, lunch, work: Every day so far is exactly the same at Oak Glen Primary School, except when there is a fire drill. At least at Magdalena we got to do different things, like art and music. At Oak Glen, art and music are considered frills.

Hah.

X X X

After school is finally, finally over for the day, Cynthia and I walk across the patio together. I think she has forgiven me about this Friday. If my mom is making me stay home, it's not *my* fault I can't go over to her house, is it?

I have almost forgotten that this is not the truth.

I am walking Cynthia only as far as the street. Mr. Harbison is coming to pick Cynthia up from school, but I get to walk home today.

The wind is blowing a little, and in spite of everything, I am happy to be outside—because even when Ms. Sanchez opens the windows in our class, it smells like floor wax, disinfectant, sweaty feet, and old tuna sandwiches in there.

But outside, I feel as though the wind could blow me all the way home. Maybe I'll even skip part of the way—if no one is watching, that is. Because the kids at my new school might think that skipping is babyish.

"Hey, look," Cynthia says, and she stops and points.

Oh, no.

There, underneath a pepper tree, are Mom and Anthony.

They are not supposed to be here.

Mom and Anthony point back at us, and then they start smiling and waving as if spotting us is the high point of their afternoon. Cynthia and I walk up to them. I feel like a fish that Mom has just caught and is reeling in. I am doomed, even though I am fake-smiling like crazy.

"Hi, Mrs. McGraw," Cynthia says.

"Hello, Cynthia," my mom says, giving her a hug. "How cute you look today. This is our little friend Anthony," she adds, introducing him to Cynthia.

Anthony blushes and ducks his curly black head, which has a raggedy red construction-paper fireman's hat on it. This is his way of saying hello to Cynthia, I guess.

"Yes, I heard all about him," Cynthia says, sounding like a grown-up. She looks Anthony up and down as if she is inspecting him, and he steps back, alarmed.

"I was just picking Anthony up from preschool," Mom is explaining, "and we thought it would be fun to wait for you, Emma. Want to join us for some ice cream? You're welcome to come, too, Cynthia, if you're free." Mom gives Cynthia a great big smile.

"I can't. My father's picking me up today," Cynthia says.

"Oh. Too bad," Mom says.

I look around, trying to find Cynthia's navy-blue car in a hurry. I have a very bad feeling

about Mom and Cynthia talking together when there is a lie floating around in the air.

"So, what did you two girls decide about Friday?" Mom asks Cynthia.

"Huh?" Cynthia asks.

Because I told her everything was decided.

"Oh," my mom says, smiling. "I guess things are still up in the air. But it would be nice if you could come over to our house and help out with Anthony, Cynthia."

Cynthia doesn't even look at me. Her mouth makes a straight line on her face, as if a pencil just drew it there. "I'm sorry, Mrs. McGraw, but I can't come over," she tells my mom. "I have to play with my cat that night. I'm going to be very busy."

Just then, a horn beeps, Cynthia spots her father's car double-parked in front of the school, and she runs off, her shiny hair swinging.

"That girl forgot to say good-bye," Anthony says, straightening his paper hat. "She isn't very polite."

7

triceratops

"Okay," Mom says to me when we get home, after feeding a *Cartoons & Songs for Little Buckaroos* video into the VCR for Anthony. "What's going on here?" She leads me into the kitchen and pours me a glass of milk.

"What's going on where?" I ask her, looking around, but I know what she is talking about.

She's talking about Cynthia, that's what.

"What's going on with your new friend Cynthia Harbison?" she asks, sure enough.

I take a slo-o-o-ow drink of milk, then I look up at her. "I told her a widdle fib," I say, trying to say it cute, like Elmer Fudd.

"You *lied?*" Mom practically squawks.

See, that's the trouble with my mom—you can't fool her by saying things cute.

"What did you say to her, Emma?" Mom asks me.

I give a big sigh. "Okay. I told her that you said I couldn't go over to her house this Friday. I said I had to stay home and help you babysit Anthony."

"Emma, I told you that you *could* spend the night at Cynthia's, if that's what you really wanted to do," Mom says, snapping out the words.

"Yeah, but you didn't mean it," I say. "You wanted me to stay home."

Mom scrunches up her face. "Well, maybe I did," she admits, "but I left the final decision up to you."

Thanks a lot, Mom.

"So, why did you decide to stay home with us on Friday?" Mom finally asks me.

"I don't know," I mumble. We both listen to Anthony for a minute. We can hear him shouting out a song, along with the video. "Maybe I feel a little bit sorry for Anthony," I say.

"He misses being at his own home," Mom says, nodding.

"And he is kind of fun to be around," I surprise myself by saying. "You never know what is going to happen next with him."

"You're right about that," Mom says, laughing. "Do you know what he did this morning, when I was trying to work?"

See, my mom has an office at home now. Instead of being a librarian for a big company, like before, she corrects books for writers, kind of like an extra-fancy English teacher. Words are her *business*. That's probably why she's so fussy about them.

"No, what did he do?" I ask her.

"He got into my hair gel, and he turned himself into a triceratops. Used up the whole tube,"

Mom says. She makes a *too-bad-but-it-was-worth-it!* face. "I should have suspected something was up, he was so quiet."

"Did you take a picture of him for me?" I ask her.

"No film," she said, shaking her head sadly.

"Well, next time, take a picture," I tell her.

But then we look at each other, because—because we both know that there probably won't *be* a next time. Anthony will be going home pretty soon.

I am surprised that I feel a little bit sad about this.

Mom sighs. "I always wondered what it would be like if you had a little brother or a little sister, Emma," she says softly. She has a mushy look on her face. As I said before, my mom and dad got divorced a long time ago, so there weren't any more babies.

My father lives in England, so I don't get to see him very often. But he and his new wife haven't had any babies. And I haven't ever met her, but I can't imagine a person with a fancy name like Annabelle changing anyone's diaper.

Of course, I could be wrong.

"It would be crowded and noisy if I had a little brother or sister," I say, having now had some experience. "But it would also be kind of fun, at least some of the time," I add, thinking of splashing, singing, crying, peanut-buttery Anthony.

"Lots of fun," Mom says, brightening a little bit. "But tiring," she adds, her eyes suddenly big and serious. "Very tiring." She rubs her neck.

"I know what you mean," I say. I take a dainty sip of my milk and try to look like a grown-up lady who is also tired.

Mom giggles again. Then she says, "So, what

are you going to do about lying to Cynthia?"

Wham, I am a kid again. "It wasn't exactly a lie," I say.

"Yes, it was," Mom tells me. "And what are you going to do about it?"

"Um, hope she forgets it ever happened?" I suggest.

"She won't forget. Not Cynthia," Mom says.

My mom is right about that, I think.

I stare at the top of the table. "I guess I'd better say I'm sorry," I tell Mom at last.

"That's my girl," Mom says, smiling.

"Okay. I'll do it tomorrow, at school," I say.

"You'll do it tonight," Mom informs me. "Poor Cynthia," she adds, making a sad face that is intended to urge me toward the phone. "How do you think she's feeling right about now?"

How am *I* supposed to know how Cynthia is feeling? What am I, a mind reader? Knowing how Cynthia gets when she is angry, though, I figure that she is probably biting the heads off animal crackers, or blowing bubbles and then popping them, or yelling at her cat, or something like that. I don't say this to my mom, though.

But my mother is not waiting for an answer to her question. "Why don't you use the phone in my bedroom when you call her," she tells me. "You'll have more privacy that way."

"Okay," I say, taking the hint. I get up from the table. "Um, are you going to punish me? For telling a fib? I mean a lie. *A lie*," I say, correcting myself in a hurry.

My mom laughs. "I think you've already been punished enough, Emma," she says. "You should have seen the look on your face when Cynthia found out that you hadn't told her the truth. It was priceless." And she actually smiles.

"Huh," I say.

"No," Mom says, half to herself and half to me. "I don't think you'll be lying again anytime soon."

I don't think so, either, but she doesn't have to

Zoos feed flamingos shrimp to keep them pink.

be so cheerful about it. So I just stalk out of the kitchen like a flamingo, without saying another word.

Flamingos are pink from eating shrimp, did you know that? Not from blushing, of course.

Anyway, I am not looking forward to this telephone call.

% % %

Unfortunately, Cynthia is home when I call her. She even answers the phone. "Don't hang up," I tell her. "It's me."

"Me, who?" Cynthia says coolly.

Uh-oh, I think, *this is going to be even harder than I*

thought. She is going to make me crawl. "Me, Emma," I tell her. "Don't hang up," I say again.

She doesn't hang up, but she doesn't say anything to me, either.

I clear my throat. "Okay, listen," I say. "I'm sorry I lied to you—I'm *really* sorry, I mean. My mom said I could make up my own mind about Friday, but I just didn't know what I wanted to do. And then when I knew, I was afraid to tell you."

"How come you didn't want me to come over to your house?" Cynthia asks. "Because you didn't want to share that little boy with me?"

"Huh?"

"Sharing that little kid," Cynthia says,

explaining. "Like we were real babysitters," she adds. "You know, teenagers."

That's what Cynthia wants to be when she grows up: a teenager. She told me.

"I don't think you would like Anthony, once you got to know him," I tell Cynthia. "I mean sure, he's cute and everything, and he can make a pretty good fireman's hat out of construction paper, but he also wrecks toys. And he hogs the VCR, too, and he drools when he sleeps."

"We could train him not to drool," Cynthia informs me.

Now, this is a weird thing for her to say. *Train* him? Like a seal in the zoo, or something? "I don't think Anthony would be that easy to train, Cynthia. And anyway, he's just staying with us for a week. We wouldn't get very far."

"Then Friday night is our only chance to try. We'll pretend we're teenagers, and we'll babysit, and we'll teach him how to do stuff," Cynthia says.

"You—you mean you really *want* to come over on Friday?" I ask her.

"Well, yeah, if it's okay with your mom. And with you," she says, suddenly shy.

"It's okay with both of us," I tell her, only half telling the truth.

Cynthia gets all excited. I can hear it even over the phone. "Oh, Emma," she says, "we can play school with him, and pick out clothes for him to wear, and dress him up, and everything."

"Uh-huh, uh-huh," I say, going along with all of Cynthia's goofy plans. Over the phone, anyway.

She will find out the truth about Anthony soon enough.

But at least we are friends again—until we attempt to babysit Anthony Scarpetto on Friday night, anyway.

x 8 x

Scissors Skills

"Can you watch Anthony for about forty-five minutes?" my mom asks me that night, right after dinner. "I've got to catch up on some work— uninterrupted, for a change. I've gotten a little behind."

"I've got a little behind, too," Anthony says, shaking his bootie and dancing around the kitchen.

I think he actually made a joke, but I decide to ignore it. My mom starts to giggle, though.

"*Watch* him?" I ask my mom. "All by myself?"

This would be Cynthia's dream come true, I guess.

"I'll still be here, Emma. I'll just be busy working," my mom reassures me. "All you have to do is to play with Anthony for a little while."

"O-o-o-kay," I say reluctantly.

"Now, stay out of trouble, you two," my mom says playfully, preparing to make her get-away. "Don't squabble, and don't try to cook anything."

"What about the chain saw?" I call after her as she disappears down the hall. "Can we use the chain saw, Mom?"

"What's a chain saw?" Anthony asks.

"I don't know. Something loud and scary," I tell him, looking at my watch.

Not even one minute has gone by. That means we have more than forty-four minutes to go until my mom stops working and starts taking care of Anthony again.

"What do you want to do?" Anthony asks, looking sort of lost. He is no longer shaking his little behind, I notice.

"I don't know. Something safe," I tell him.

That eliminates doing puzzles, for one thing.

"I could take a bath," Anthony says.

"Nope. Too dangerous. But I could read you a story," I tell him, quickly trying to figure out which of the old picture books in my room would make him sit still the longest.

"Nope. Too dangerous," Anthony says, grinning at me.

I grin back, and then I look at my watch again. I sigh. "Well, what about drawing some pictures?" I ask, mentally crossing my fingers— because drawing is something that might keep Anthony quiet the whole time Mom is working.

"What kind of pictures?"

"Anything! Pictures for your mom and dad," I say, inspired. "And one for your grandmother in Tucson."

"Okay," Anthony says, brightening. "But you draw, too."

"If you insist," I say, and I get the crayons and paper out of the kitchen cupboard where Mom keeps our art supplies.

This could actually be fun! It's been a long time since I used crayons.

Anthony flashes me a sunny smile, and we set to work.

X X X

Forty-three minutes later, my mother comes into the dining area and plops a plastic bag on one end of the table.

Anthony throws his crayon down, jumps off his chair, flings himself against my mother's legs, rubbing his pink and white face into her skirt. He is acting as if he thought she would never walk back into the room.

She doesn't topple over, for once. I think she

is getting used to Anthony.

"Hey," I tell him. "Don't make such a big deal out of everything. It's not like you've been locked in a closet. We were having fun, remember? *Coloring?*" I wave my hand toward the table. Its surface is 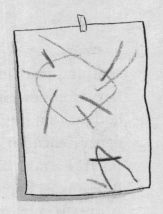 almost covered with ten or eleven of Anthony's spidery drawings.

He works fast.

"Yeah," Anthony says, his voice muffled. "But don't go away again, okay?" he begs my mom, looking up at her face. Right on schedule, tears trickle down his cheeks.

"Oh, honey. Of course I won't," my mother says, her voice breaking with emotion as she sinks to her knees. She gathers him into her arms. "I didn't know it would upset you."

"It *didn't* upset him, not until now," I tell my mom. "He was perfectly fine."

"Well, never mind," my mother says in a soothing voice as she attempts to unstick Velcro Boy from her legs. "I just remembered that I bought you guys some brand-new construction paper when I went to Office Depot this afternoon. Sorry I didn't think of it sooner, Emma. But I was hoping that you and I could help Anthony cut some up."

"Cut some up?" I echo. Buying colored paper and then cutting it up sounds like a waste of money to me.

And my mom is usually so careful about every penny she spends.

"Miss Becky says my scissors skills are weak," Anthony says, looking tragic.

Mom and I both bite our lips and try not to smile, hearing such an unusual sentence come out of little Anthony's mouth. But I guess that bad scissors skills are nothing to laugh about if you're four years old. And I don't want Anthony to flunk out of preschool!

"Well, let's get cutting," I say, starting to stack up Anthony's drawings.

"Wait—I haven't signed my art yet," Anthony says, reaching for an orange crayon.

Now, first of all, his drawings are not exactly masterpieces. No one is going to mix them up with the art I did tonight, for instance: pictures of perfectly shaded birds. And for another thing, all of Anthony's drawings look exactly the same. He could sign one, and everyone would get the general idea. And third, since it takes Anthony about ten minutes and a tongue sticking out of his mouth to print even his first name one time, it is clear that there are not enough hours in the day for him to sign every piece of art he dashes off.

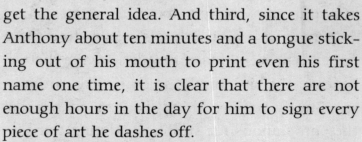

I try to think of some quick way to distract

him, but my mom beats me to it. "Careful! Very sharp scissors," she says, popping a brand-new pair of blunt-nosed scissors out of their snug plastic covering and handing them to Anthony.

She bought those for him, too!

But because of the look on Anthony's face, I'm not even a little bit jealous or mad. I whisk his drawings into the living room and put them on a high shelf while he is still staring greedily at the scissors.

He is exactly like a magpie! They are interested in bright, shiny objects, too.

A magpie is a bird that is similar to a crow, but even noisier. In fact, magpies are the chatter-boxes of the bird family, so that's like Anthony, too. But the funniest thing about magpies is that they are famous for stealing glittering things—watches, keys, little pieces of metallic paper—

and hiding them in their nests. They don't need the things they take, obviously, but they *want* them.

I can totally understand that. Not that I'm about to start stealing things. But sometimes you see something, and you find yourself thinking, *If I only had that, everything would be okay.*

I feel that way when I see other people's families. They seem so—so solid.

I could never tell my mom that, though, because it's been just her and me for the last six years, and she makes this big deal out of *us* being a family.

And I completely agree! I mean, if two people is all there are, then that's your family.

But when I was coloring with Anthony tonight, it felt almost like a *real* family. The living room clock was ticking, and Anthony was humming Christmas carols under his breath,

Magpies can imitate the human voice.

and I heard Mom's printer whirring, and the crayons smelled good, and I could still smell the tacos my mom cooked us for dinner, and for one floaty moment, I was completely happy.

I wasn't wishing for something more.

The strange thing is, nothing about tonight was different from any ordinary night—except that Anthony Scarpetto was here.

Maybe that's the difference. When I'm alone with Mom, it's just us hanging out, and it's always her taking care of me. But with Anthony here, *I* get to have someone to take care of, too.

He's only four, and he's lonely, and he needs me.

"Cat got your tongue?" Mom asks me, snipping construction paper into little pieces.

This is something she says when I am being unusually quiet.

I smile. "Nope. Tonight, a *magpie* has my tongue," I tell her, and I select a piece of paper to cut up and then throw away.

"Magpie, magpie, magpie," Anthony whispers, concentrating so hard on his own piece of paper that he doesn't even ask what the unfamiliar word means.

Which is highly unusual, and not very educational for him.

But that's okay. At least his scissors skills are improving.

a teeNsy LittLe fight

"Where is he?" Cynthia asks on Friday night. She is standing at the front door. Her shiny hair is pulled back tight by a red plastic headband, the kind with little teeth in it. And she is holding onto a suitcase with a picture of ballet shoes on the side. The suitcase is round, and it is shiny, too.

Everything Cynthia owns always looks brand new.

"He, who?" I ask, but I already know the answer. She is talking about Anthony.

"You know," she says, excited, "that little kid. The one we're babysitting." She pats the side of

her suitcase. "I brought some stuff we can use," she says. "We can play school with him. We'll be the teachers."

"He's watching a video right now," I tell Cynthia. "And I'm not so sure about playing school. He had a tough week. I think he needs a rest from school."

"Well, that's just too bad for him," Cynthia informs me. We go into my room, and she puts her red suitcase down on my bed. She and I are going to sleep on the living room floor tonight, though, in sleeping bags. Anthony will be the only one staying in my room.

Cynthia walks over to my guest bed and looks at all of Anthony's stuff: his inside-out sweatshirt, his giant Legos, his new blunt-nosed scissors, his stuffed bunny rabbit.

I don't like her spying on his private things.

"Let's play dolls," I say to her. That's what we usually play when she comes over, even though we don't talk about it at school, since we don't want to sound babyish. "Which one do you want to be?" I hold up my newest doll. She is wearing short shorts and tiny Rollerblades, and her hair is almost as shiny as Cynthia's.

Last time, we fought over this doll. But not today.

"Let's go get Anthony," Cynthia says.

"Well, maybe we should wait until after dinner," I say. I was hoping she would forget her crazy plan about playing school with Anthony. "Come on, let's play dolls," I say again, tempting her with the short shorts, Rollerblade doll with shiny hair.

But Cynthia just walks right out of my bedroom as if I haven't said a word.

This is a whole new Cynthia, I think, following her.

We walk past the kitchen, where Mom is fixing dinner. "Hello, Cynthia," she calls out. Her voice is all smiley, as if she thinks this is going to be a really fun night.

"Hi, Mrs. McGraw," Cynthia says, barely looking at my mother. She just keeps right on walking— like a Bengal tiger stalking its prey.

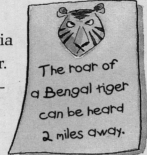

The roar of a Bengal tiger can be heard 2 miles away.

Anthony is sitting in the most comfortable chair in the living room. A little blanket is spread across his lap, as if he is about to have a picnic. I can tell that he would like to be sucking his thumb. I have noticed that he does that sometimes, when he is really, really tired.

I can also tell he is a little sad, only no one else but me would know that. But he's not even singing along with the video this afternoon, and he knows it by heart, naturally.

"Hi, Anthony," I say. "This is Cynthia, remember?"

Anthony's eyes shift sideways for a second, then he nods his head. "I remember," he says.

I cross my fingers, hoping he does not add the

part about how he does not think that she is very polite. Because she *is* polite. Oh sure, she gets mad fast, but already I have learned that her anger goes away fast, too. And after it goes, Cynthia is ready to have fun again.

I think that's better than staying a little bit mad for a long time, which is more like what I do. My mom says I'm a kid who really knows how to hold onto a grudge.

"Hello, Anthony," Cynthia says, sounding like a teacher already. "Do you want to play school with us?" she asks him. "It'll be fun."

"Nuh-uh. That's okay," Anthony says. He stretches his neck, trying to see around Cynthia—who is standing right in front of the TV. If he were in the third grade, like us, he would probably say, "*Move! You make a better door than a window,*" the way EllRay Jakes does at school.

I still don't really get that. Why would any-one want to be a door *or* a window?

Cynthia tries again. "I brought some fun little prizes for you," she says.

"Move it," Anthony says, still trying to see the TV.

"That's not very courteous," Cynthia informs him. I can tell that she does not like it that things aren't going her way. "We're going to have to teach you some manners, young man," she says, sounding sniffy.

"Okay, *please* move it," Anthony says to her. I can also tell that Anthony is getting mad.

Uh-oh, I think. I am the only calm person in the living room—and even *I* am not feeling so calm anymore. "Listen," I say to Cynthia, trying to make things peaceful again, "why don't we play school with Anthony after dinner?"

"Shhh," Anthony says, staring at the video. "I can't hear what they're saying."

"We should play *now*," Cynthia tells me. "He'll be too tired later. And you shouldn't let little kids have their own way when they're being bad."

And she grabs the remote from the table, punches its one red button, and turns both the TV and VCR off.

"Hey," Anthony yells, and he tries to jump up from the chair. His legs get tangled in the little blanket, though, and he crashes to his knees.

"Horses eat hay," Cynthia informs him, the very second that he starts to cry.

Ms. Sanchez says, *"Horses eat hay"* whenever one of us kids in her class says, *"Hey."* That's where Cynthia got it from.

"Horses? So what?" Anthony is yelling, just as my mom rushes into the living room. Mom is holding a wooden spoon straight up in the air as if she is an insect with only one antenna.

"Anthony, what happened?" Mom asks him. "Did you fall? Are you hurt?"

"Cynthia and Anthony are just having a teensy little fight," I tell her. "It's no big deal."

"That not-nice girl made me fall off the chair," Anthony says between big sobby gulps— ignoring me. He points his blaming finger at Cynthia.

"It's rude to point," Cynthia says, as though she is reciting a rule that everybody knows. But her voice is a little bit quieter now, because my mom is in the room.

"Point, point, *point*," Anthony says, jabbing his finger at her again.

"Anthony, darling, calm down," Mom says to him.

Cynthia takes a deep breath. "Yes," she says, pointing at Anthony now. "*Sit*. And *stay*."

Just as if Anthony was a cocker spaniel or something!

I can't help it—I start to giggle.

Mom starts chuckling, too.

But not Anthony, and not Cynthia. Now they are both angry—with *us*. "Stop it," Anthony says, putting his little hands on his little hips.

"Yeah, quit laughing," Cynthia says, but to me, not to my mom. "I thought we were friends, *Emma*," she adds, scowling.

"We—we—we are," I say, trying to catch my breath. "You just sounded funny, that's all."

"I did not," Cynthia says.

"*Sit. Stay*," I say, pointing at Anthony. I am pretending that I am Cynthia, so she can see for herself how silly she sounded.

"No," Anthony yells at me.

"Bad dog," I yell back.

Now, Cynthia is the one to giggle—she can't help it!—but then she turns her laugh off suddenly, as if it were a radio someone had turned on by mistake. She glares at me, even angrier now. "Hmmph," she snorts, and she flops down into a chair. She folds her arms, scrunches up her face, and starts looking at the wall, even though there is nothing there.

And Anthony is madder than ever, too.

If that is even possible.

"*Yah–h–h*," he howls, and he runs out of the living room and down the hall.

Mom and I stare at each other. I think each of us is wondering, *What just happened?*

And then, just when you would think that nothing more could go wrong, the doorbell rings.

❧ 10 ❧

No fair!

Even though the bell jingles and jangles, Mom and I stand very still, the way animals do when they don't want anyone to notice them. "It's probably the police," I tell Mom. "I guess our

neighbors heard all the yelling and everything. You can't make a lot of noise when you live in a condo, remember."

"Oh, Emma," Mom says. But it's as if my words have released her from a magic spell, because she runs to open the front door.

And Anthony's mother is standing there.

She came home early. No fair!

"Surprise," she says, holding out her arms as though she knows we will be happy to see her. "I tried to call from the airport," she says, "but—"

"Mommy!" Anthony shouts, hearing her voice, and he whizzes down the hall and throws himself into her arms.

"Little bunny rabbit," Anthony's mother says, and she bursts into tears while she is hugging him.

I guess that's where Anthony gets his crying skills from.

They *Mommy* and *Little-bunny-rabbit* back

and forth a couple of times more. You would think that my mom and I had been making Anthony's life miserable, the way he is clinging and carrying on.

You would think I hadn't been playing with him—more and more each day, actually. And enjoying it, too.

I sneak a peek at Mom. We are both looking a little bit lonelier already.

"Can you stay for dinner?" my mom asks Anthony's mom. "It's almost ready."

"No. Jack's out in the car with the motor running," Anthony's mom says, standing up.

Mom gives her a worried look. "Well, I hope that Anthony's grandmother—"

"Complete recovery. Happy ending in Tucson," Anthony's mom says, smiling.

Mom sighs. "Well," she says, "let me get this little guy's things together. It will only take a minute."

"Could I stop by tomorrow, instead, to pick

up his gear?" Anthony's mom asks. "We're just so anxious to get home. I know you understand."

Home. To our old neighborhood. Just the three of them.

I understand, anyway.

In fact, I kind of wish I could go with them.

"But I want my bunny *now.* And my blanket," Anthony says, and he trots off down the hall. He comes out of my bedroom with the stuffed rabbit—whose head is practically falling off, it has been kissed and slobbered on so much— and he goes into the living room for his blanket.

And I suddenly remember: *Uh-oh. Cynthia's still in there.* I had forgotten all about her. So I go into the living room, too.

"Here," Cynthia is saying, holding out the raggedy little blanket to Anthony.

"Okay, thanks," Anthony says back, businesslike, as he scoops it into his arms.

"I'm sorry if I was kind of bossy," Cynthia says to him.

See, that's another good thing about Cynthia: She says sorry when she is wrong.

I hate doing that.

"You were a *lot* bossy," Anthony informs her. "But that's okay," he adds, waving his rabbit in the air as if he is using it to say *I forgive you.*

Sure, he can be nice to her now, because he is leaving!

Right before he walks out the door, he turns around, runs back to me, and gives me a big old hug. "Bye, Emma," he says. "See ya."

I don't say anything. I just squeeze him back.

X X X

After Anthony and his mother are gone, Cynthia, my mom, and I sit down for dinner. We are having spaghetti, Anthony's favorite. I give a big sigh and slurp up a few noodles in his honor.

The three of us are pretty quiet.

When dinner is finished, Cynthia and I wander back into my bedroom. Mom has already taken the used sheets off Anthony's bed so she can wash them. That's one good thing! Cynthia and I can sleep on regular beds tonight, in my own room.

So everything is back to normal, except for the part about me missing Anthony.

Cynthia dumps her little round suitcase out onto my bed. She looks at the markers she brought for playing school with Anthony, and the paper, and the prizes she brought for him: a granola bar and an eraser shaped like a goldfish.

I want that cute eraser. "You can play school with me," I tell Cynthia.

"It's not the same," she says, shaking her head. She picks up the granola bar, though. "Want to to split it?"

"Sure," I say, and so we do.

11

Here is What i think

It is Saturday morning. After breakfast, Cynthia and I are sitting on the little wall in front of the condo, waiting for Cynthia's father to come pick her up. She turns to me and asks, "So, what was it like, anyway, having a little brother?"

"He wasn't really my brother. And I only had him for five days," I say.

"But what was it like?"

I think for a minute. "Well, I hated it at first," I say, remembering. "And I never really *loved* parts of it. Not the mess and the noise, or watching my mom give him presents and hugs. And everything in the house got sticky, and the VCR

was always blaring away, and my whole room smelled like peanut butter after a couple of days. But I don't know, I kind of got to really like Anthony."

"How come, when he wouldn't even play right?" Cynthia asks. She is frowning as if she is trying to do subtraction at the board, which is the hardest kind. In front of other people, I mean. "You couldn't make that kid do anything," she reminds me.

"Yeah, but I didn't *want* to make him do stuff," I tell her. "I just got used to having him around, I guess—doing nothing. I like him," I say again.

I look down the road. Maybe Anthony and his mom are on their way here now, to pick up the rest of his stuff. I kind of hope they don't come until Cynthia is gone, though. Because Anthony and I would have more fun without her being here.

"Huh," Cynthia says, as if that is not the

answer she was looking for. "Well, I like being an only child. I would hate it if my mom and dad had another kid," she adds, smoothing her hair back.

It is already smooth, though. It always is.

"Well, I like being an only child, too," I say, even though I am not as sure about this as I was a week ago.

Just then, Cynthia's father drives up in his navy-blue Audi. So she says good-bye to me, and away they go.

But I stay on the little wall, in the shade.

⅗ ⅗ ⅗

Here is what I think: The good parts about being an only child are that nobody messes with your toys and stuff, and you get to watch what you want on TV, and your mom gives lots of every-thing—hugs, toys, attention—just to you.

The bad thing about being an only child is—
no Anthony. Only Emma.

Oh, sure, I guess I will get used to being alone
again. I will probably even like it. But for right
now . . .

Yuck.

She may not admit it, but saLLy waRNeR was a little like Emma when she was young, and a lot like Emma's mother when she had children of her own. Dubbed the "queen of kids' comedy," by *The Buffalo News*, she lives with her husband, a sculptor. They both work at home and are supervised by their miniature wirehaired dachshund, Rocky.

Please visit her at www.sallywarner.com.

⁊ ⁊ ⁊

jamie HaRPeR thanks her three daughters for all the inspiration they provided for her illustrations. None of her daughters are just like Emma, but they would like her as a friend. Ms. Harper is also the author and illustrator of *Don't Grown-Ups Ever Have Fun?* and *Me Too!* She and her family live near Boston, Massachusetts.

Please visit her at www.jamieharper.com.